IMAGINE THAT™

Licensed exclusively to Imagine That Publishing Ltd
Tide Mill Way, Woodbridge, Suffolk, IP12 1AP, UK
www.imaginethat.com
Copyright © 2018 Imagine That Group Ltd
All rights reserved
2 4 6 8 9 7 5 3
Manufactured in China

Written by Susie Linn
Illustrated by Rosie Butcher

ISBN 978-1-78958-6107

A catalogue record for this book is available from the British Library

Cinderella

Written by Susie Linn
Illustrated by Rosie Butcher

Once upon a time, there lived a girl whose mother had died and whose father had married again. The new wife and her two daughters were very mean to the girl, who was forced to cook, mend, wash and iron all day.

At night, the girl slept by the fire's glowing cinders,
so her ugly stepsisters called her ...

Cinderella.

One day, a letter came from the royal palace.
'The prince has invited us to a royal ball!'
shrieked one of the ugly stepsisters.

It was an invitation to all of the young ladies in the kingdom.
At the end of the night the prince was going to choose his bride!

The day of the ball soon arrived and the stepsisters were very excited.
As they put the final touches to their outfits, Cinderella asked her
stepmother what she might wear.

'You're NOT going to the ball!'
laughed her stepmother and stepsisters, cruelly.

Poor Cinderella felt upset,
so she ran outside and cried.
But just then ...

... a fairy appeared out of nowhere!

'I'm your fairy godmother,' the fairy said, kindly.

With a flick of her magic wand, the fairy godmother transformed a nearby pumpkin into a beautiful carriage!

She changed two mice into horses!

Then she transformed a rat into a coachman and two lizards into footmen!

Finally, she turned Cinderella's scruffy dress into a beautiful ballgown, and birds fluttered down with a pair of glass slippers.

'*Enjoy the ball,*' said the fairy godmother.
'*But, make sure you're back home by midnight,
or the spell will be broken!*'

Cinderella thanked
her fairy godmother
and set off to the ball.

The palace looked magical in the moonlight and Cinderella was very excited. No one in the room recognised her, and everyone agreed that she was the most beautiful young lady at the ball!

The prince was enchanted by Cinderella's beauty and he danced with her all night. As the clock crept slowly towards midnight, Cinderella was having such a wonderful time that she forgot to leave!

DONGGG!

DONGGG!

DONGGG!

Suddenly, the clock struck twelve
and Cinderella remembered what her
fairy godmother had said.

Without a word, Cinderella fled and vanished into the night,
leaving one of her glass slippers behind on the palace stairs.

The prince picked up the glass slipper
and called out to his helper.
**'Go and search the kingdom for the girl
whose foot fits this slipper! She is the girl I
wish to marry!'**

The weeks passed, and the prince's helper searched
the whole kingdom, until only Cinderella and
her ugly stepsisters were left.

The first ugly stepsister tried to
squeeze and push her foot into the
slipper, but no matter how hard she
tried, her foot was too big.

Then the second ugly stepsister tried the slipper on, but her foot was too small.

'No luck here!' exclaimed the prince's helper, and he turned to leave.

'Wait!' cried Cinderella's father. 'I have a daughter.'

The stepmother and the ugly stepsisters looked at him in disbelief!

'Her? She didn't go to the ball!' shrieked Cinderella's stepmother.

'Hmm ...' thought the helper, looking at Cinderella. *'She seems familiar.'*

And with that, Cinderella slipped her foot into the glass slipper ... and it fitted perfectly!

Cinderella travelled nervously back to the palace,
but she did not need to worry. The prince recognised
her at once as the beautiful girl he had danced with.

'*Will you marry me?*' he asked Cinderella, taking her hand.
'*Yes!*' said Cinderella joyfully. Cinderella and the prince were married
the very next day, and they lived happily ever after.